Jem the Fowey Pirate

Jennifer Bell

Illustrated by Simon Goodway

JEM THE FOWEY PIRATE

Jennifer Bell

Illustrations by Simon Goodway
simon@simongoodway.com

ISBN: 978-0-9934032-3-1

This book is published by Jennifer Bell in conjunction with WRITERSWORLD, and is produced entirely in the UK. It is available to order from most bookshops in the United Kingdom, and is also globally available via UK based Internet book retailers.

WRITERSWORLD
2 Bear Close Flats, Bear Close, Woodstock
Oxfordshire, OX20 1JX
England
☎ 01993 812500
☎ +44 1993 812500
www.writersworld.co.uk

The text pages of this book are produced via an independent certification process that ensures the trees from which the paper is produced come from well managed sources that exclude the risk of using illegally logged timber while leaving options to use post-consumer recycled paper as well.

This book belongs to

Jem the Fowey Pirate

Jem was bored.

His parents were working so he was staying with his grandfather in Readymoney Cove for the summer.

Now his grandfather was busy and it had started to rain.

He sat on the floor and looked through
the bookcase.

He found a book called *Pirate Adventures*.
It looked exciting.

"I know", he cried. "I'll dress up as a
Pirate and have an adventure."

He found a pair of his grandfather's red sailcloth shorts.

He pulled the belt tight and swaggered around.

He found his striped top and knotted a cotton handkerchief round his head.

He looked in the mirror. He was pleased.

"I look just like a pirate," he said. "Now I'll go and rob people of their treasure."

He rowed his boat out into the harbour and pulled in front of a family in a motor boat.

"Stop," he cried. "I'm Jem the Pirate. Stop and give me your treasure."

The family on the motor boat looked at him and pointed and laughed.

"He thinks he's a pirate but he doesn't fool anyone. He's just a boy dressed up."

They motored on.

"I just don't look fierce enough to be a pirate," thought Jem sadly, so he went to see the boat builder.

The boat builder looked around his yard.

"I have a dragon figurehead, a red sail and a Jolly Roger. These will make you look like a pirate."

When the boat was finished, Jem was very pleased. He looked up at the Jolly Roger and smiled."This looks just like a pirate ship," he cried. "Now people will be very frightened and they'll stop and give me their treasure.

So he rowed his boat out into the middle of the harbour
and pulled in front of a racing yacht.

"I'm Jem the pirate" he cried. "Stop and give me your
treasure!"

The sailors looked at him and pointed.

"He thinks he's a pirate," and they all laughed.

"Get out of our way or . . . .

"We'll run

Poor Jem. He wanted to be a pirate so much and no one would believe him.

He walked along the beach and felt very dejected.

Then he saw a long, knobbly stick that had been washed up by the tide. He picked it up.

"I can be very fierce and I can swash-buckle with this," he cried, whirling the stick above his head. "Now they'll believe I'm a pirate."

He rowed again into the middle of the harbour and saw a large, tourist boat full of holiday makers.

He pulled his boat in front of them and brandished his knobbly stick.

"Stop!" he cried, "I'm Jem the pirate. Stop and give me your treasure."

The tourists rushed to the side of the boat to see Jem. They laughed so much that the boat capsized and they all fell into the water.

"Help! Help!" they cried.

"This way, swim to me, grab my stick," and one by one Jem pulled them onto his boat.

Jem took them to shore where they climbed the steps and shivered in their wet clothes and shook his hand crying, "Thank you, thank you. You saved our lives!"

The harbour master saw all this through his window and thought, Jem deserves a medal for rescuing all those people.

A few days later everyone came to the town quay.

The lifeboat men gave Jem a guard of honour.

The brass band played and all the people clapped as the harbour master presented Jem with the Fowey Town Medal. Jem smiled at his grandfather, watching from the steps, and thought he must be the happiest boy in all Cornwall.

Jem decided that it was much better to help people rather than frighten them.

He put away his pirate clothes, his red sail, his Jolly Roger and his knobbly stick.

He kept the figurehead, though – the dragon was really cool.

For the rest of the holiday, Jem rowed his boat round the harbour, looking out for boats in trouble,

And sometimes, when there were no boats around,

he caught a few fish for supper.

CMP (UK) Ltd. Sales Office: 960 Capability Green • Luton • LU1 3PE
Factory: G3 The Fulcrum • Vantage Way • Poole • Dorset • BH12 4NU
Switchboard: 01202 739993 www.cmpbookprinting.co.uk

By the same author, to be published in 2016

Stories for Grandparents and Other Children:

Left Behind

The story of a house martin too young to join the Autumn Migration.

The Little Christmas Tree

A small tree struggles to grow in a rocky crevice by the water's edge and longs to be chosen as a Christmas Tree.

Twonk

Oliver's turtle, Twonk, suddenly speaks and tells Oliver a story of slavery and the 'Night People'.

Ouch!

A crab's daunting experience of the summer holidays in a rock pool.

About the author

Since making up stories for my little sister I have collected a cupboard full of writing - mainly for children. Now retired, I am enjoying tackling this pile of paper and finding stories to publish. This is a new challenge and great fun!

In this story, set in Fowey, in Cornwall, children will enjoy recognising Tom's Boatyard in Polruan, the Harbour Master's steps in Fowey, and the Town Square where Jem is presented with his medal.

Readymoney Cove, the setting for grandfather's cottage, is a great beach for children and families and has a scenic scramble up to St Catherine's castle from which, in the old days, a chain was fastened across the harbour entrance to repel invading French ships.

A variety of boats are to be seen in the harbour – ships going upstream to the larger berths to collect exports of china clay, visiting cruise liners, all sorts of leisure craft and tourist boats, and, of course, Demelza.